The Case of the Clubhouse Thief

Look for these Clue™ Jr. books!

The Case of the Clubhouse Thief

Book created by Parker C. Hinter

Written by Della Rowland

Illustrated by Dan DeLouise

Based on characters from the Parker Brothers game

A Creative Media Applications Production

SCHOLASTIC INC.
New York Toronto London Auckland Sydney

No part of this publication may be reproduced in whole or in part, or stored in a retrieval system, or transmitted in any form or by any means, electronic, mechanical, photocopying, recording, or otherwise, without written permission of the publisher. For information regarding permission, write to Scholastic Inc., 555 Broadway, New York, NY 10012.

ISBN 0-590-86634-6

Copyright © 1997 by Hasbro, Inc. All rights reserved. Published by Scholastic Inc. by arrangement with Parker Brothers, a division of Hasbro, Inc. CLUE® is a registered trademark of Hasbro, Inc. for its detective game equipment.

12 11 10 9 8 7 6 5 4 3 2 1   7 8 9/9 0 1 2/0

Printed in the U.S.A.

First Scholastic printing, February 1997

Contents

Introduction

Meet the members of the new Clue Club. Samantha Scarlet, Peter Plum, Greta Green, and Mortimer Mustard.

These young detectives are all in the same fourth-grade class. The thing they have most in common, though, is their love of mysteries. They formed the Clue Club to talk about mystery books they have read, mystery TV shows and movies they like to watch, and also, to play their favorite game, Clue Jr.

These mystery fans are pretty sharp when it comes to solving real-life mysteries, too. They all use their wits and deductive skills to crack the cases in this book.

You can match *your* wits with this gang of junior detectives to solve the eight mysteries. Can you guess who did it? Check the solution that appears upside down after each story to see if you were right!

1

The Case of the Made-up Test

"**A**re you feeling any better, Peter?" Greta Green called out to Peter Plum. Greta was standing in the school yard with Samantha Scarlet and Mortimer Mustard, waiting for the bell to ring. Peter walked across the school yard toward his friends from the Clue Club. He had been absent from school for several days with the flu. This was his first day back.

"Yeah, I'm all better," he replied glumly. "But now I have two tests to make up. And one of them is today!"

"What subject?" asked Samantha.

"Math, my worst subject," Peter wailed. "I think I'm getting sick again!"

"Don't worry," said Mortimer. "I'll help you study at lunch." Mortimer was a straight-A student.

"Thanks, Mortimer," said Peter. "Now my lunch is spoiled, too."

Everyone laughed. "Oh, grow up, Peter," said Greta. "A little studying isn't going to kill you."

During lunch, Mortimer helped Peter study and showed him a trick for remembering long division rules. When the bell rang, Peter said, "Thanks, Mortimer. I hope I can remember all this."

"We'll wait for you after school, Peter," said Samantha. "After you make up your test, we'll go for pizza to celebrate."

"Great," sighed Peter. "At least I'll have that to look forward to."

After school, the Clue Club kids all stood outside Ms. Redding's door waiting for her to tell Peter to come in for his test. Also waiting was one of the Allbright twins. Amanda and Anna Allbright were in Ms. Redding's class.

"Are you Amanda or Anna?" asked Samantha.

"Amanda," the girl laughed.

4

"Sorry, Amanda, but I still can't tell you two apart," laughed Samantha.

"Neither can I," admitted Peter. "Especially when there's only one of you."

"The only way I can tell you apart is that you're right-handed and Anna is left-handed," said Mortimer.

"Don't feel bad," said Amanda. "Sometimes our own parents can't tell which is which."

"Are you making up a test, too?" asked Peter.

"Yeah," Amanda answered. "Math."

"Uh-oh," said Greta. "Isn't that your worst subject?"

"No, it's my best," said Amanda.

All the kids looked surprised. "Since when?" said Mortimer.

"Just kidding," laughed Amanda. "It's Anna's best subject."

"Don't confuse me," Samantha said with a smile. "That's one way I can tell you two apart."

"I'm sorry," said Amanda. "I didn't mean

any harm. Sometimes I just can't help fooling people. It's a lot of fun."

"I'd love to be able to do that," said Peter, "especially right now."

Everyone stopped laughing when Ms. Redding came to the door. "All right, you two," she said to Amanda and Peter. "Come on in and let's get started."

"Or finished," muttered Peter under his breath.

"You'll do fine," said Mortimer. "Just remember the trick I showed you."

After a while, the kids peeked into Ms. Redding's class to see how Peter was doing on the test.

"Peter looks pretty worried," said Greta. "I'll bet he doesn't remember your trick."

"Well, Amanda looks like she's doing okay," said Samantha.

"All right," said Ms. Redding. "Time to hand in your tests. If you want to wait a few minutes, I'll grade them now."

"Great," said Amanda. "I'll wait."

"Uh . . . I guess I'll wait, too," said Peter hesitantly.

The kids sat down in the empty seats to wait for Ms. Redding to grade the two tests. After a few minutes, she said, "Not bad, Peter. You got an eighty-one."

"Wow!" whooped Peter. "That's great!"

"Amanda, you must have studied very hard," Ms. Redding said. "I don't think you've ever gotten a hundred on a math test before. Congratulations!"

"Gee, Amanda," said Peter. "I studied all lunch period with Mortimer the Great Brain and I did a little better than usual. But you usually do worse than me. How'd you do it?"

"I know how she did it," piped up Mortimer. "She cheated."

Why does Mortimer think Amanda cheated?

Solution
The Case of the Made-up Test

"Why, Mortimer, what a thing to say," exclaimed Ms. Redding. "Explain yourself."

"I think Anna took the test, not Amanda," said Mortimer.

"How can you tell?" asked Greta.

"Oh, I know," cried Samantha. "Anna is left-handed. When she and Peter were taking the test, she was sitting on his right side."

"Right. And the hand she was writing with was the one closest to him," said Greta.

"Which means it was her left hand," said Mortimer.

"Anna!" exclaimed Ms. Redding. "Shame on you. You almost got away with cheating for your sister. Well, you take this note home to your parents telling them why Amanda got a zero on this makeup test. I'll have to speak to them about this."

"This makeup test turned out to be a made-up test," laughed Peter.

The Case of
the Cave Painting

"**N**ow this is the way to spend a school day!" exclaimed Peter. He and the Clue Club kids were lined up with the rest of Ms. Redding's fourth-grade class waiting to board a school bus. They were headed for the Hobart Natural History Museum for a field trip. Mr. Easel, the art teacher, was taking the class to see the museum's show on cave paintings.

When they arrived at the museum, Mr. Easel led them to a room that the museum had set aside for them.

"You can hang up your coats on the coat-rack, and put your lunches on this table," Mr. Easel announced. "After we see everything, we'll come back here and eat lunch."

"I hope my bag doesn't wind up on the

bottom of the pile," said Samantha. "I hate squashed sandwiches."

"Never had a squash sandwich," said Peter. The three friends rolled their eyes at Peter's lame joke.

"Let's go, class," said Mr. Easel. "The slide show's about to start."

The slide show began with a time line that showed the different periods when animals and humans lived. Mr. Easel stood by the screen while he pointed out different eras.

"As you can see in this time line," he said, "even though dinosaurs were already extinct, the cave people had to deal with some pretty fierce animals like the saber-toothed tiger and the woolly mammoth. Now let's see how those animals show up in their cave paintings." He flipped the slides to display cave drawings of human figures fighting different animals — one was of a woolly mammoth, and another was of a bison. Then Mr. Easel showed slides of

other things the cave people painted —
horses, suns, and clubs.

After the slide show, the students
walked through the wing of the museum
that had cases of early human bones and
pieces of weapons. They looked at diora-
mas that depicted how early people lived.
One showed a replica of a caveman about to
throw a spear at a saber-toothed tiger.

"We're going to the gift shop now," said
Mr. Easel. "Then we'll head back to the
room where we left our lunch bags."

When they reached the room, the class
discovered that someone had gone though
all the lunch bags and opened drinks and
taken bites out of sandwiches, apples, and
candy bars.

"Who did this?" Mr. Easel demanded. No
one answered. "Well, only one person left
the room during the slide show," he said.
"That was Samantha, who was excused to
use the rest room."

"Me?" cried Samantha. "I wouldn't do
anything like this."

"Samantha, I'm surprised. This isn't like you," said Mr. Easel. "Your parents will have to come in after school to discuss this."

"What am I going to do, guys?" wailed Samantha to the other Clue Club kids after the class had returned to the bus. "I didn't do it!"

"Unfortunately, there's no way to tell if anyone else left during the slide show," said Mortimer.

"Yeah," said Peter. "The room was dark and you're the only one who asked to be excused."

"Don't worry, Samantha. We'll find a way to figure out this mystery and prove you're innocent," said Greta.

Back at the school, Mr. Easel asked the students to color their own cave paintings. While they were at work, he put up the time line that was used in the slide show, which he had bought at the gift shop. Finally, everyone was finished.

"Let's show our paintings to the rest of

the class," said Mr. Easel. "Jimmy, Sandra, and Mortimer, go to the front of the class and hold up your cave paintings."

As Jimmy, Sandra, and Mortimer held up their paintings, Mr. Easel checked his watch. "Uh-oh, class, I've just noticed that the bell is about to ring," he told everyone. "We'll look at your cave paintings tomorrow; but for now, just put them on my desk as you leave. Samantha, remember I'd like to see you after school. Maybe we can get to the bottom of your mysterious behavior."

Peter held up his hand. "Mr. Easel," he said. "I have another suspect for the lunch bag mystery."

"You do?" said Mr. Easel.

"Yes. It's Jimmy," said Peter.

Why does Peter think Jimmy messed up the lunch bags?

"And since you missed that part of the show, you could have sneaked outside and ruined our lunches," said Peter.

Caught in a lie, Jimmy confessed and the mystery was solved.

"Thanks, Peter," said Samantha. "That was a good catch."

"Yes, you can color Jimmy caught," laughed Peter.

Solution
The Case of the Cave Paintings

"And why do you think it was Jimmy?" asked Mr. Easel.

"Because I don't think he saw the slide show," said Peter.

"How could you know? It was too dark to tell if anyone left," said Mr. Easel.

"If he had seen the slide show he would have drawn a different cave painting," said Peter. Everyone looked at Jimmy's painting.

"I see what you mean, Peter," said Greta. "His scene couldn't have happened."

"What do you mean?" cried Jimmy. "What's wrong with this scene?"

"Dinosaurs were extinct way before humans were around," said Mortimer.

"That's right," said Mr. Easel.

"You would have known that — if you had seen the slide show," said Samantha. "It made such a big deal about it, you couldn't have missed it."

The Case of the Missing Mittens

Greta called Samantha early one Saturday morning in a panic. Her cat, Mittens, was missing. "I haven't seen her since last night," said Greta.

"Don't worry," Samantha said. "I'll call the rest of the club and we'll be right over. We'll find your furry friend."

Samantha called Peter and Mortimer and they hurried over to Greta's house. In twenty minutes, they were all gathered around the kitchen table to hear what happened.

"Mittens disappeared last night and hasn't been back," Greta told them. "Not even for food. It isn't like her to miss any meals. I'm really worried."

"Last time I saw her, Mittens didn't look

like she'd been missing any meals," said Mortimer.

"Yeah," agreed Peter. "I think she's been putting on weight."

"Well, that's true," said Greta. "She has been eating more lately."

"Let's check your room first to see if Mittens left any clues behind," said Peter.

"Good idea, Peter," said Samantha. "Mittens usually sleeps on Greta's bed."

The kids climbed the stairs to Greta's room. "I haven't made my bed yet," Greta said, straightening her covers. "When I woke up this morning and Mittens wasn't sleeping with me, I started looking for her right away."

"It looks like she was here," said Samantha. "Seems like she tried to make a little nest out of your comforter."

"Yeah, she did that yesterday, too," said Greta. "She's been messing up my bed all week."

"Look," said Peter, pointing to some

dirty paw prints on the comforter. "Mittens left something for you." He giggled.

"Oh, no! Mom'll kill me," cried Greta. "Wait a minute. I don't think these tracks were here when I got up. Maybe Mittens came in here this morning. Boy, this is really getting to be a mystery."

Just then Greta's mom walked by her room carrying an armload of sweaters and winter pants. "I'm sure Mittens will turn up, sweetheart," she told Greta. "It's not unusual for cats to disappear from time to time, you know."

"Doesn't Mittens like to go outside?" asked Mortimer.

"Yeah," answered Greta. "But she never stays out all night, especially when it's cold. And the weather has been getting colder."

"Speaking of cold weather," Mrs. Green said, "I've gotten the last of your winter clothes out of the attic. I'll put them on your bed and you can hang them up. Deal?"

"Okay, Mom," Greta said. After her mother left she told the others, "My mom stores our clothes in the attic. All day yesterday she was carrying summer clothes up to the attic and this morning she's been carrying winter clothes down."

"Sounds like she's getting carried away with clothes," giggled Mortimer.

A few minutes later Mrs. Green poked her head in Greta's room once more. "Oh, Greta," she said. "Speaking of missing Mittens, I couldn't find your winter mittens. I must have stuck that box in the back of the attic. Could you take a look? My back is bothering me and I don't want to crawl around up there."

"Sure, Mom," Greta answered. "Come and help me, guys."

The Clue Club kids climbed the creaky attic stairs. When they opened the attic door, Greta flipped on the light switch at the top of the stairs. Nothing happened. "I guess the bulb is burned out," she said.

"There's enough light coming through the window," said Samantha. "I think we can see okay."

"Let's look over here," said Greta, leading the kids to the back of the attic. "This is where my mom usually puts the clothes."

"Watch out," said Mortimer, waving his hands around his head. "Cobwebs."

The kids were crawling around looking for the box of mittens when they heard the stairs creaking. "Mom?" called Greta. There was no answer. "Mom!" she shouted. No answer. "That's creepy," she said, standing up.

Then they heard a rustling sound and squeaking noises coming from the back of the attic. "Something's back there," hissed Mortimer. "And it's moving."

"And it's making noise," said Samantha.

"Mittens," Greta called out. "Here, kitty, kitty." When no cat appeared, she said, "I guess it's not her. She always comes when I call."

"So what is it?" said Samantha. "A mouse?"

"Whatever it is, it's alive," said Mortimer, shivering.

"Let's get a flashlight and see," suggested Peter.

"Good idea," said Mortimer, heading for the stairs.

Samantha was right behind him. "And a lightbulb," she said. "It's kind of dark in here."

The four kids scurried down the stairs. Greta found a lightbulb in the pantry and got a flashlight from a kitchen drawer.

"Look," said Mortimer, pointing to the cat's food dish on the floor. "Some of Mittens's food has been eaten."

"Well then, where is she?" said Greta. "This is too weird."

Mortimer spotted some doughnuts on the kitchen table and hinted that he'd love to have a snack before they headed back to the attic.

"Of course, Mortimer, but everyone wash your hands first," Mrs. Green told them. "Look how dirty they are."

"I guess it's from crawling around in the attic," said Greta.

Suddenly Samantha's eyes opened wide. "Wait!" she exclaimed, smiling. "I'll bet I know where Mittens is."

"Where?" cried Greta.

"Where she got her paws dirty," said Samantha mysteriously.

"Outside?" asked Peter.

"No, the same place we got our paws dirty," said Samantha. "The attic."

"You mean that *was* Mittens making that noise?" said Mortimer.

"No," answered Samantha. "It's something else. Come on. I'll show you."

How does Samantha know Mittens is in the attic? And what is making the noise?

for them with your comforter," explained Samantha. "Then your mom left the attic door open when she was storing clothes. That's when Mittens came up here and made a bed for her kittens."

"That's where she disappeared to last night," said Mortimer.

"And she went down to eat when your mom opened the attic door this morning to get the rest of the winter clothes," said Peter.

"Hey," said Peter. "It looks like we found all the lost mittens. And they were all in one box!"

Solution
The Case of the Missing Mittens

Samantha led everyone back up the stairs to the attic. "She's over there," she said, pointing to the corner where the noise was coming from.

"Okay, I'll get her," said Peter, crawling back into the corner.

"How did you know she was coming up here, Samantha?" asked Greta.

"You'll see," Samantha answered.

Just then Peter crawled out from the corner of the attic, pulling a box marked MITTENS on the side. The top was open and inside were several pairs of winter mittens and woolen scarves. Lying among them were Mittens and three tiny kittens.

"So the noise we heard wasn't coming from Mittens," said Mortimer. "It was Mittens' new kittens."

"That's why she was gaining weight!" exclaimed Greta.

"At first she was trying to make a bed

The Case of the Birthday Bang

"**I** can't wait until Saturday," Samantha told the Clue Club kids Monday as they walked home from school.

Saturday was Samantha's birthday and her parents were taking her and the club to the bowling alley for a party.

"Let's get some pizza," said Mortimer. "I'm starving."

"What else is new?" laughed Peter. "You're always starving."

As the kids headed for the pizza parlor, they saw Patsy Pinto, a classmate, walking their way.

"Hi, Patsy," called Samantha. Patsy ignored her.

"Is Patsy still bent out of shape because she wasn't invited to the birthday party?" asked Greta.

"Yeah," sighed Samantha. "I explained to her a jillion times that my parents will only let me invite a few friends."

The kids caught up with Patsy. "Patsy, don't be mad," said Samantha.

"I thought you were my friend," Patsy said to her. "You're nothing but a snob."

"But I told you," Samantha explained. "My parents put a limit on guests. Otherwise the party will cost too much. Believe me, you're not the only friend I couldn't invite."

That just made Patsy even madder. She glared at Samantha then stormed off.

"What's her problem?" said Mortimer. "That's happened to me plenty of times."

"Me too," said Peter. "I mean, no parents are going to let their kids invite as many friends as they want to a party."

For the rest of the week, Patsy wouldn't speak to Samantha. Finally, on Friday, Patsy apologized to Samantha. "I'm sorry I got mad," Patsy said. "I don't want to ruin your birthday."

"I'm glad you understand," said Samantha. "Listen. I'm having cake and stuff at my house after the party. Can you come?"

"Sure," said Patsy. "See you tomorrow."

On the day of the party, Samantha and the other Clue Club kids were in the middle of a bowling play-off when Patsy showed up with some of her friends.

"Patsy!" exclaimed Samantha, surprised. "What are you doing here?"

"Happy birthday, Samantha," Patsy said. "Listen, I can't come over later, so I brought you your birthday present now. Come over here where I can give it to you."

"Oh, thanks, Patsy," said Samantha. "You didn't have to do that." Samantha told her parents she'd be right back and followed Patsy and her friends into another room. A bowling team was having a celebration there for winning the county championship ten years in a row.

"Come over here," Patsy said, pointing to the table on which a tall bowling trophy

was standing, "by that table." As Samantha headed for the table, Patsy suddenly screamed. Everyone in the room turned to look at her. Just then several of the large decorative balloons in the room began popping.

"What was that?" shouted Patsy.

Samantha's parents and the Clue Club kids ran over to her. "What's going on, Samantha?" said her dad.

"I'm not sure," replied Samantha. "All of a sudden all these balloons started popping."

The bowling alley owner pushed through the crowd. "What happened here?" he shouted.

One of the women on the bowling team stepped up. "These girls came in our room, and then one of them started popping our balloons," she told him angrily.

"These balloons were made up especially for the team," said another woman.

"You'll have to replace them," a man told

the girls. "And they aren't cheap, you know."

"She did it," accused Patsy, pointing to Samantha.

"Me?" cried Samantha.

"I saw her poke them with a pin," insisted Patsy. "I'll bet the pin is on the floor right around here."

The owner bent down and picked up a big safety pin. "Yep, here it is," he said, holding it up for everyone to see. "What were you girls doing in here in the first place?" he asked.

"Don't ask me," said Patsy. "I brought Samantha a birthday present but she didn't want to open it around her other friends. I guess she's ashamed to be seen with me. Maybe that's why she didn't invite me to her party. Anyway, she wanted to come over here to open the present. I didn't understand why until now. I guess she wanted some special sound effects on her birthday."

"I think Patsy is responsible for the noisemakers," said Peter.

"Oh, you do, do you?" said Patsy. "Well, it's your word against mine. *And* my friends'." Her friends nodded to show they agreed with Patsy.

"No, you did it, and I can prove it," said Peter.

How does Peter know Patsy is lying?

Solution
The Case of the Birthday Bang

"You did two things that gave you away," said Peter. "One, you screamed before the balloons popped."

"So?" said Patsy.

"The only reason you would scream before they popped is if you knew what was going to happen," replied Peter. "I think you wanted everybody to be looking at Samantha when the balloons got popped."

"You mean that's how she got everyone's attention," said Mortimer.

"Maybe I saw her doing it, and that's when I screamed, smarty," said Patsy.

"Then why did you ask what happened if you already knew?" said Greta.

At that, Patsy was trapped. "All right," she admitted. "I popped the balloons. I'm still mad at Samantha for not inviting me to her party so I decided to ruin it for her."

"Well, I'm going to give both parties an extra hour of free time to make up for this girl's prank," declared the bowling alley owner. "And now we'll call your parents and figure out what to do with you."

"Patsy tried to pull a birthday joke on you, Samantha, but you had the last laugh," said Peter with a grin.

5

The Case of the Clubhouse Thief

It was spring and it was Saturday — the best kind of day. Peter, Samantha, and Greta were on their way to Mortimer's house. The regular Saturday morning Clue Club meeting was being held at his house that week.

"The sun feels so good," sighed Samantha as they walked along. She stretched up her arms. "Now I think I know how a plant feels."

"I don't know about that," said Peter, "but I sure do want to be outside today. Maybe we should have the meeting in the park."

"I'm for that," said Greta. "Let's run it by Mortimer when we get there."

When they arrived at Mortimer's house, he announced, "I have a surprise." He led them outside into the backyard and pointed to his clubhouse. "It's finally warm enough to have the Clue Club meeting in the clubhouse," he said.

"Great!" exclaimed Peter. "Now we can be inside and outside, too."

When everyone was inside the clubhouse and ready to start the meeting, Peter announced that he had a surprise, too. He pulled a new poster out of his backpack.

"Wow!" exclaimed Samantha. "It's a Moving Target poster!"

"Cool!" said Greta. "Those are hard to find."

"I know," Peter said, beaming with joy. "I've been checking at the comic store every day for a month. This one finally came today."

"You want to hang it in the clubhouse so we can look at it while we have our meeting?" said Mortimer.

"Sure!" said Peter.

Peter carefully positioned the poster on

a wall of the clubhouse. "Is it straight?" he asked the others.

"Yep," said Mortimer. "And now let's call this meeting to order." The kids discussed how they could raise some money to purchase a mystery movie that had just come out on video. After they took care of some other business, they got out their Clue Jr. game.

"Hey, all this work is making me hungry," said Mortimer. "Let's head inside for some lunch." No one had to be asked twice. The kids piled into Mortimer's kitchen where a plate of sandwiches was waiting for them.

While they were eating they saw a boy run past the kitchen window. He ran across the backyard and into the house just behind Mortimer's. "Hey!" exclaimed Samantha. "That was Bob Blanch, wasn't it? Doesn't he live in back of you, Mortimer?"

"That's right," Mortimer answered.

"Why was he running through your yard?" said Greta.

"Don't worry," said Mortimer. "He uses our yard as a shortcut all the time because his house is right in back of ours."

"Listen," said Samantha, "let's play some more Clue Jr. in the clubhouse."

"Okay with me," said Greta. Peter and Mortimer agreed. They put their dishes in the sink and headed outside again.

When the kids walked back into the clubhouse, Peter saw right away that his poster was missing. "It doesn't take Sherlock Holmes to figure out that Bob took it," he fumed.

"Well, I don't know," said Mortimer. "Why don't we go talk to him?"

"When we get to Bob's house, let's just tell him we're coming for a visit," Samantha whispered. "We don't want him to suspect that we suspect him."

When they rang Bob's doorbell, he answered the door and invited everybody inside. "This is a surprise," he said. "What are you guys up to?"

Peter picked up a comic book catalog

that was sitting on a table beside a chair. "I just got a new comic book hero poster today but now I can't find it," he told Bob.

"That's too bad because Moving Targets are rare," said Bob. "But it will turn up. It's probably somewhere in your house. Half the things I lose are right under my bed."

"I'll bet you could help Peter find his poster," said Samantha.

"Sure, I guess so," said Bob. "But why me?"

"Because you took it," Samantha responded.

How does Samantha know Bob took Peter's poster?

Solution
The Case of the Clubhouse Thief

"What do you mean I took it?" cried Bob.

"It's pretty obvious," Samantha told him. "How did you know which poster was missing?"

"That's right," said Mortimer. "Peter just bought it today."

"The only way you would know who was on the poster is if you saw it," said Greta.

"Oh, okay," Bob sighed. "I went into the clubhouse to see if you guys were there. When I saw the poster, I just took it. I don't know why."

"That really isn't like you, Bob," said Mortimer.

"I know, Mortimer," Bob said. "The poster is in my room. I'll get it for you, Peter?" Bob went to his room, came back with the poster, and handed it to Peter.

"Moving Target sure lives up to his name," laughed Peter. "He really moves around."

The Case of the
Wild-Goose Chase

Friday evening, Peter told Samantha, "Mortimer and Greta are meeting me at my house at seven-thirty tomorrow morning, but we'll pick you up about quarter to eight. That way you can sleep a little while longer."

"Seven-thirty!" Samantha gasped. "On Saturday?"

Peter laughed. Samantha loved to sleep late on the weekends. She got very upset if she had to wake up before ten o'clock. But tomorrow Mr. and Mrs. Plum were taking the Clue Club kids to Farmer Fowle's Petting Farm. They wanted to get an early start.

"See you tomorrow, Samantha," Peter told her.

The next morning, when the Plums

pulled up to Samantha's house, she was sitting on her front porch yawning and rubbing her eyes. As soon as she got inside the car, she promptly fell back asleep and didn't wake up until they had arrived at the farm.

"Wake up, Samantha," said Mrs. Plum. "We're here."

"Yeah, Samantha. Can't you hear the rooster crowing?" snickered Peter.

"Look, there are Kevin and Alex," said Mortimer.

"Where?" said Samantha, perking up. "Oh, yeah. And there are Francis and Nell and Julie." She pointed to some more of their classmates who were also there with their parents.

Altogether, there were about twenty people visiting the farm that day. After the group had settled down, everyone gathered around Farmer Fowle, who was leading the tour. He explained that the kids could touch all the animals — except where there were signs, like on the bull pen.

"All the animals are used to people," he

told them. "I only ask that you don't feed them anything unless we give it to you. And of course, don't annoy them. They're like any other creatures. They like to be treated with respect."

First the group visited the barnyard. Dozens of chickens and chicks were scratching in the dirt for worms and bugs. Ducks and geese were waddling to and from the nearby pond. The kids peered inside the chicken house where the chickens roosted at night.

"Are those straw nests where the chickens lay their eggs?" Samantha asked Farmer Fowle.

"That's right," he answered. "We collect them once every day and sometimes twice. If you notice, some of the nests have eggs in them now." He lifted up a chicken and showed the children an egg she was sitting on.

"Do you collect duck eggs, too?" Francis asked Farmer Fowle.

"Not really," replied Farmer Fowle. "They don't lay as many as chickens do."

Then he became serious. "Be very careful around the geese," he warned. "They can be grouchy sometimes and might try to peck at you. My advice is, don't cross a goose or your goose is cooked," he laughed. "Now let's go inside the barn where large animals are kept."

Inside the barn, the children climbed up into the hayloft where straw for the animal stalls was kept. "It's the animals' mattresses," said Farmer Fowle.

When they climbed down, Mortimer poked Peter with his elbow. "Where did everyone go?" he whispered.

"A bunch of kids had to go to the bathroom," Peter answered.

"Great!" fumed Mortimer. "Francis was holding my camera for me, and now I want to take some pictures of the animals."

"What's a mule?" one kid asked. "It sort of looks like a horse."

"It sort of *is* a horse," answered Farmer Fowle. "It's a cross between a horse and a donkey."

"Why do you cross a horse with a donkey?" asked another kid.

"Because mules are stronger than donkeys," replied Farmer Fowle. "By the way, Millie here is a male."

The group laughed. "Then how did he get the name Millie?" asked Mr. Plum.

"Well, my daughter named him," chuckled Farmer Fowle. "When she was three she couldn't say 'mule,' so she called the animal 'mill.' We just got to calling him Millie after a while."

The kids walked around to the stalls to pet two horses named Horace and Patty, a Shetland pony named Pony Tail, and Mildred the milk cow. "Mildred is pregnant," Farmer Fowle told the group. "In fact, she's going to give birth any minute."

"She looks pretty big," said Greta.

"Speaking of big, look how big those horses are!" said Peter.

"Horace and Patty are Clydesdale horses," said Farmer Fowle. "They are very strong, and bred to pull heavy wagons with big loads."

"At last! Here come the other kids," said Mortimer, pointing to the stable door. "Where's my camera, Francis?" he whispered loudly.

"Ssssh!" hissed Francis. "Here's your stupid camera. Hold it yourself."

"Well, we're off to see the pigs now," said Farmer Fowle, leading the group out the barn door. Just then, one of the farmhands came to tell him that Mildred had started to give birth.

"Right-o," said Farmer Fowle cheerfully. "Children, I've got to see to Mildred. I'll see you before you leave. Thank you all so much for coming and please go on with your tour. My son Harry here will help you."

Harry led the group to the pigsty, which was a fenced-in area below the barnyard. "Meet Sowsie," said Harry, pointing to a huge pig lying on her side in the middle of the sty. "She's the mother of all these piglets."

Suddenly there was a ruckus near the barn. Two boys were running down the hill toward the pigs. Several geese were honking and squawking and chasing them.

"'Look! It's Kevin and Alex!" cried Peter. "The geese are chasing them!"

"Stand back, children!" shouted Harry. "Remember what we told you about geese. Let me handle this." He took his straw hat and ran between the boys and the geese, shooing the great, angry birds away with the hat and speaking in soothing tones to them. Finally, the geese retreated.

"Whew! Those geese were mad," said Harry. "What happened?"

"We were on our way to see the pigs," began Kevin.

"And all of a sudden the geese attacked us!" wailed Alex.

"Hmm," said Harry. "These geese are so

used to humans that they wouldn't chase you unless they got riled for some reason. You boys didn't do anything to upset them, did you?"

"No way," said Alex.

"They just started after us!" cried Kevin.

"Well, the reason I ask is because I noticed eggs splattered on the geese," said Harry.

"Which reminds me, where have you boys been?" asked Kevin's father.

"In the barn," said Kevin. "When we heard Farmer Fowle say that Mildred was having a baby, we wanted to watch a mule being born."

"Well, that's a relief. I'd hate to think of anyone in this group picking on the animals here," said Kevin's father.

"Excuse me," said Samantha. "I'm afraid they might have been picking on the geese."

"Why do you say that?" asked Harry.

"Because I know they weren't in the barn watching Mildred give birth," answered Samantha.

Why does Samantha think Kevin and Alex are lying?

Kevin and Alex looked at each other.

"Okay," said Alex. "While everyone was in the barn, we went into the chicken coop to swipe some eggs. Then we threw the eggs at the geese on our way to the pigsty."

"We thought it would be more fun to throw eggs at the geese than to look at some stupid pigs," said Kevin. "We didn't know the geese would chase us like that."

"I hate to say this, but it serves you right, son," said Kevin's dad.

"I guess a goose doesn't have to be wild to give someone a good chase," laughed Peter.

Solution
The Case of the Wild-Goose Chase

"What are you talking about, Miss Know-It-All?" shouted Kevin. "Isn't Mildred having her baby?"

"Yes," said Samantha. "But Mildred isn't a mule."

"I thought Millie was a nickname for Mildred," said Alex.

"It is," said Mortimer. "But Mildred is a cow, not a mule."

"And the mule couldn't have a baby anyway," giggled Greta. "Millie the mule is a male!" Everyone burst out laughing.

"It's pretty obvious that you guys weren't in the barn when Farmer Fowle was explaining all this," said Samantha. "So you didn't hear him say that Millie was a male," said Mortimer.

"Plus you didn't know Farmer Fowle has a Mildred and a Millie," said Peter. "Why don't you guys tell us the truth now?" said Harry.

The Case of the Changing Money

It was a hot summer day, a perfect day to set up the lemonade stand. The Clue Club kids mixed up several pitchers of lemonade in Greta's kitchen and carried them out to the stand. Carefully, they lined up the cups on the counter next to the pitchers. Then they hung up a sign they had made. It read COLD LEMONADE — 5¢ A GLASS.

"Now we're set," said Greta, smiling. "Help me carry some folding chairs out so we can sit down between customers." The kids carried out chairs and Mrs. Green handed Greta a shoe box covered with dollar signs. "Here, Greta, a money box for your profits."

"Profits," said Mortimer, looking at the box and smiling. "What a nice word."

"I say we take the profits and get ice

cream," Samantha said. Everyone agreed with her splendid summer idea.

They placed their money box under the counter and sat down to wait for customers. At first just a few kids came along, but as the day grew hotter, more and more stopped. Even Mr. Post, the mailman, had a glass while he was delivering the mail.

Just before lunch, Richie Royal walked down the street. When he saw the stand, he stopped.

"I'll have some lemonade," he said. Peter poured him a glass and Richie drank it down in one gulp.

"That'll be a nickel," Peter said.

Richie smirked. "I only have a five-dollar bill. Do you have change?"

"We don't have change for a five," said Mortimer. "And I'll bet you don't even have a five-dollar bill to make change for."

"Well, you can't expect a customer to hand over all his money if you don't have enough change," Richie said, walking away.

"Ooooh, he makes me so mad," fumed Greta.

"Oh, well," said Samantha. "It's only a nickel. Forget it."

As the day got hotter, the kids got busier. Several customers came by more than once. At lunchtime Mrs. Green came out to have a glass of lemonade.

"Would you kids like to take a break and have some lunch inside where it's cool?" she asked them.

"Yes!" exclaimed Peter.

"I would, too, but I'd hate to close the stand," said Mortimer. "Business is booming."

"Let's see how much money we have first," said Samantha. She dumped out the dimes, nickels, and pennies, and they carefully counted up their profits, which came to $2.95.

"Hmmm," said Mortimer, smiling. "Business is good today."

Just then, Lenny Lilac came up. "That looks good," he said, wiping his forehead with his sleeve. "I'll have a glass." He plunked down a nickel on the lemonade stand counter.

"Sure," said Samantha, pouring him a glass. "Now we have three dollars." Everyone looked at the money on the counter.

"Can you give us three dollars for our change, Mom?" asked Greta. "It's going to be hard to carry all these coins to the ice-cream parlor later."

"Sure," her mother replied. She gave the children three one-dollar bills.

"Say, Lenny, would you watch the stand while we have lunch?" Mortimer asked.

"Oh, I don't know," said Lenny. "It's too hot. Can I have another glass of lemonade if I do?"

"Better than that," said Peter. "You can keep all the profits you make while we're gone."

"Wow!" exclaimed Lenny. "You've got a deal."

The kids put their money back in the

cash box, and went inside to eat. But a couple of minutes later, they heard shouting at the lemonade stand. When they came back out, Richie Royal was there again. He and Lenny were having an argument. When he saw the kids heading toward him, Richie began yelling at Lenny. "Why won't you sell me a glass of lemonade, kid?" he shouted. "What's your problem?"

"Hey, guys! Richie just took all the money in the cash box!" shouted Lenny. "Give it back, Richie!"

"You mean *you* took it," said Richie. "Hey, Clue nerds, you shouldn't leave all your money with somebody like this."

"Wait a minute," said Peter. "Start from the beginning, Lenny."

"Richie ordered a glass of lemonade," explained Lenny. "When I opened up the cash box to put his nickel in, he grabbed it and took all the money."

"You're crazy," snorted Richie. "Listen, I bought a glass of lemonade, then I got some change from Lenny, that's all. Now he's trying to get me blamed for the missing money he put in his pocket."

"If I gave you change, then how come I don't have your money?" hollered Lenny.

"You put it in your pocket," shrugged Richie. "If you lost it, that's your problem."

"I hate to say this, but it's Lenny's word against Richie's," said Samantha.

"Did anyone else buy lemonade, Lenny?" asked Greta.

"No," said Lenny. "No one would come with Richie standing around."

"Then you're lying, Richie," said Greta.

"Well, prove it," sneered Richie.

How does Greta know Richie took the money?

Solution
The Case of the Changing Money

"Remember?" Greta said. "We just got dollar bills from my mom. So we couldn't make change for anything."

"That's right," remembered Samantha. "We had exactly three dollar bills."

"So there's no way Lenny could have made change for Richie," said Mortimer.

"Let's see how much is in your pocket, Richie," said Peter.

Richie emptied his pocket. He had exactly three one-dollar bills, plus the nickel he had of his own.

"I guess you mystery-solvers caught me this time," Richie muttered, giving the money back.

"I guess Richie had a change of heart and gave back his change," laughed Peter.

The Case of the
Lost Time

August was almost over. Peter, Samantha, Mortimer, and Greta were trying to get in as much swimming as they could before summer ended and they had to go back to school.

"How many times have we been here this week?" Mortimer asked the others as they reached the town swimming pool. They paid their admission and walked through the turnstiles.

"Almost every day," replied Samantha. The kids walked to their favorite spot, spread out their towels, and sat down. Samantha was smearing on sunscreen when she stopped and pointed to Peter's wrist.

"Isn't that the watch you got for your birthday, Peter?" she asked.

"Yeah," replied Peter. "It's great, isn't it?"

"But why are you wearing a good watch at the swimming pool?" Greta asked. "It could get ruined by the water."

"It's okay," Peter told her. "It's waterproof."

"You're kidding," Mortimer said.

"Nope," said Peter. "Here. I'll show you." Peter took off the watch and pointed to the word *Waterproof* written on the face of the watch. "See?" he said.

"So that means you could leave it on if you went into the pool?" said Samantha.

"Yep," smiled Peter. "I've actually gone in the water with it a bunch of times before today. You guys just haven't noticed."

"Speaking of water," piped up Greta, "that's where I'm going." She headed for the pool. "Last one in is a drowned duck."

The others jumped up and followed her to the diving boards at the deep end. Peter did a perfect swan dive. Everyone in and out of the pool cheered. Not to be outdone,

Greta climbed up next and held her arms out straight as if she was going to make a graceful dive, too. Then she whooped and did a cannonball. After diving a while, the kids played volleyball in a special shallow section.

"All this diving and swimming is making me hungry," said Mortimer.

"I'm ready for something to eat, too," agreed Greta.

"Say, where's your watch, Peter?" said Samantha. "It's not on your arm."

"Oh no!" said Peter. "I guess I left it on the towel when I took it off to show you it was waterproof." But when everyone returned to their towels, Peter's watch wasn't there.

"It's not here," said Peter. "Maybe I did put it back on and it fell off."

"If someone found it they might have taken it to the lost and found," said Greta.

"Or maybe you left it here and someone took it," said Mortimer, shaking his head.

"Let's start with the lost and found," said Peter.

"We can ask the lifeguard where it is," said Samantha.

When they approached the guard's seat, they noticed he was wearing Peter's watch. Or a watch that looked exactly like it.

"Where'd you get that watch?" asked Peter.

"I've had it for a long time," replied the lifeguard.

"Is it waterproof?" Peter asked.

"You bet," said the lifeguard. "I bought this watch as soon as I got my lifeguard job this spring. I wanted a waterproof watch so I wouldn't have to worry about taking it off if someone was having trouble in the water. This way, I can dive in and help a swimmer right away."

"Can I see it?" asked Peter.

"Sure, kid," the lifeguard said. He grinned and handed the watch to Peter.

"This is my watch," said Peter, checking

the watch over. "I've worn it for almost the whole summer."

"You're nuts," said the lifeguard, snatching the watch back.

Peter turned to the other kids. "Is that my watch or what?" he asked.

"I'd say so," said Samantha.

"Give me back my watch!" hollered Peter.

"Calm down, Peter," said Greta. "I think I can prove it's your watch. Let's get the pool manager."

When the pool manager arrived, the kids explained the problem. "This lifeguard picked up my friend's watch while we were in the pool," said Greta. "Now he claims it's his."

"They're all lying," said the lifeguard. "I've worn this watch all summer. These kids are ganging up on me so they can get it. Well, it won't work."

"Can you prove this is your friend's watch?" the manager asked Greta.

"Yes," said Greta. "Peter, you and the

lifeguard show the manager where you wear your watch."

After a minute, the manager said, "Well, Little Miss Detective, it looks like you're right."

How did Greta prove the lifeguard was lying?

Solution
The Case of the Lost Time

"What do you mean she's right?" exclaimed the lifeguard.

"Just look at your wrist," the manager replied. "You claim you've worn this watch all summer. If that's the case, your skin should be lighter where your watch has been. Neither one of your arms shows a tan mark. But look at the boy's arm."

Everyone stared at Peter's arm. It was easy to see the pale band of skin around his wrist where he had worn his watch all summer. Then they looked at the lifeguard's arm. It was evenly tanned. There was no watch mark.

"If you had been sitting out in the sun all summer with this watch on, we'd see a tan mark on your arm," the manager told the lifeguard. "I'm afraid I'll have to see you in my office, young man," he went on. "I'm not sure I can trust you to work for me any longer. You've violated a very strict pool rule about stealing from guests."

"Peter, it looks like you were saved by the tan," giggled Samantha.

"Yeah," laughed Mortimer. "That guard may be a lifesaver, but Greta, you're a time-saver!"

**Amber Brown doesn't want much—
just a little credit for trying!**

AMBER BROWN
WANTS EXTRA CREDIT

BY PAULA DANZIGER

Amber is in deep trouble.
Her room is a mess, her
homework is late, and to
top it all off, her mom is
dating someone!
No matter what Amber
does, it isn't enough! Why
won't anyone give Amber
credit for trying?

**Coming in March to
bookstores everywhere**

Don't miss Amber's other adventures:
AMBER BROWN IS NOT A CRAYON
YOUR CAN'T EAT YOUR CHICKEN POX, AMBER BROWN
AMBER BROWN GOES FOURTH

AMB79